D0569074

CALGARY PUBLIC LIBRARY

AUG   2018

Silver Dolphin Books
An imprint of Printers Row Publishing Group
A division of Readerlink Distribution Services, LLC.
10350 Barnes Canyon Road, Suite 100, San Diego, CA 92121
www.silverdolphinbooks.com

Designed by Kara Kenna
Cover Design by Shaun Doniger

Copyright © 2018 Silver Dolphin Books

All rights reserved. No part of this publication may be reproduced, distributed, or transmitted in any form or by any means,
including photocopying, recording, or other electronic or mechanical methods, without the prior written permission of the publisher,
except in the case of brief quotations embodied in critical reviews and certain other noncommercial uses permitted by copyright law.

Printers Row Publishing Group is a division of Readerlink Distribution Services, LLC.
Silver Dolphin Books is a registered trademark of Readerlink Distribution Services, LLC.

All notations of errors or omissions should be addressed to Silver Dolphin Books, Editorial Department, at the above address. All other correspondence
(author inquiries, permissions) concerning the content of this book should be addressed to Silver Dolphin Books.

ISBN: 978-1-68412-377-3

Manufactured, printed, and assembled in Dongguan, China. RRD/04/18

22 21 20 19 18 1 2 3 4 5

EPPIE the ELEPHANT

(who was allergic to peanuts)

 Silver Dolphin

Written by **Livingstone Crouse**

Illustrated by **Steve Brown**

Our story begins
on the first day of school
with one eager new student
and one simple rule:

"No peanuts," said Eppie.
She knew it by heart.
And she knew that to break it
wouldn't be very smart.

One whiff of peanut,
and her nostrils would twitch,
her eyes fill with water,
and her ears start to itch.

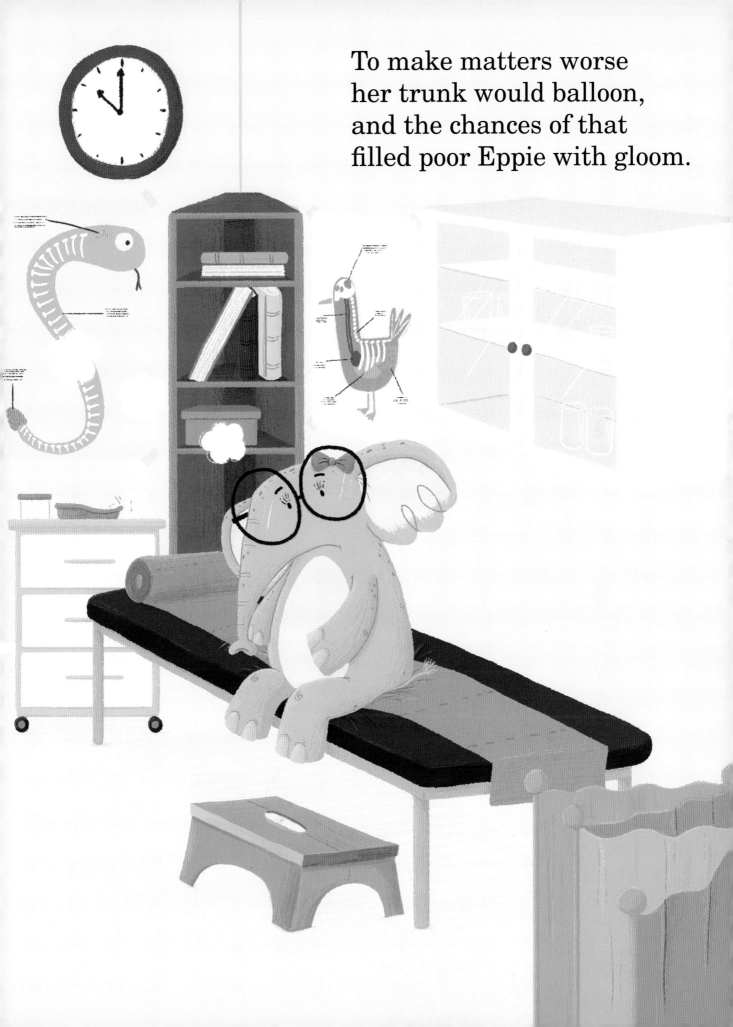

To make matters worse
her trunk would balloon,
and the chances of that
filled poor Eppie with gloom.

Of course, there were things
beyond getting sick…
Like the other kids laughing
Or thinking: "It's a trick!"

Or perhaps they'd be able
to see at first glance
that Eppie was different,
and not give her chance.

So while her teacher'd been told
and the school nurse alerted,
Eppie still feared a crisis
could not be averted.

Thank goodness her father
saw something was wrong.
He knelt close and whispered,
"You're brave and you're strong."

Hugging her tight, he said,
"You make me so proud."
He kissed Eppie's forehead
then left with the crowd.

Squaring her shoulders,
Eppie held her head high,
and bravely stepped forward
because big girls don't cry.

All that she needed was
one friendly face—
then maybe, just maybe,
things would fall into place.

Setting her course
with no time to dally,
she looked for a seat—
that's when she saw Allie.

"Oh, no!" panicked Eppie.
The moment of truth!
But Allie just grinned
showing each snaggled tooth!

"I found you a seat.
It's right here next to mine."
He sounded so hopeful
that she could not decline.

Maybe Allie didn't notice
all the eyes turning to stare,
but one thing was for certain,
Eppie made her first friend right there.

Allie even asked her
for help stacking blocks.
They built quite a city
filled with towers and docks!

And when an alphabet puzzle
gave them cause to worry,
Pearl stepped in to help
and it was solved in a hurry.

Soon they were inseparable:
Eppie, Allie, and Pearl!
And the rest of that morning
passed by in a whirl!

Come lunchtime, the trio
were bound both fast and true.
They stuck to one another
as if bonded with glue.

But just as the playmates
found a great spot to eat,
Eppie was pointed
to a lone, distant seat.

The teacher told Allie,
"You have pb&j.
That's trouble for Eppie.
She must stay far away.

And Pearl's bag of peanuts
only makes matters worse.
One touch could send Eppie
right straight to the nurse."

Allie stared at Eppie
and Pearl did the same.
Eppie started stammering,
desperate to explain.

She said, "I'm allergic.
and peanuts make me ill."
And with that, her perfect day
took a turn, downhill.

"An elephant, allergic to peanuts?
This must be a prank!"
Allie busted out laughing,
and Eppie's heart sank.

Pearl didn't say a word.
She sat there looking scared.
While this was Eppie's gravest fear,
she wasn't quite prepared.

Miserable, she wandered off
to eat her lunch alone,
and listen to her buddies
from the distant "Nut-Free" zone.

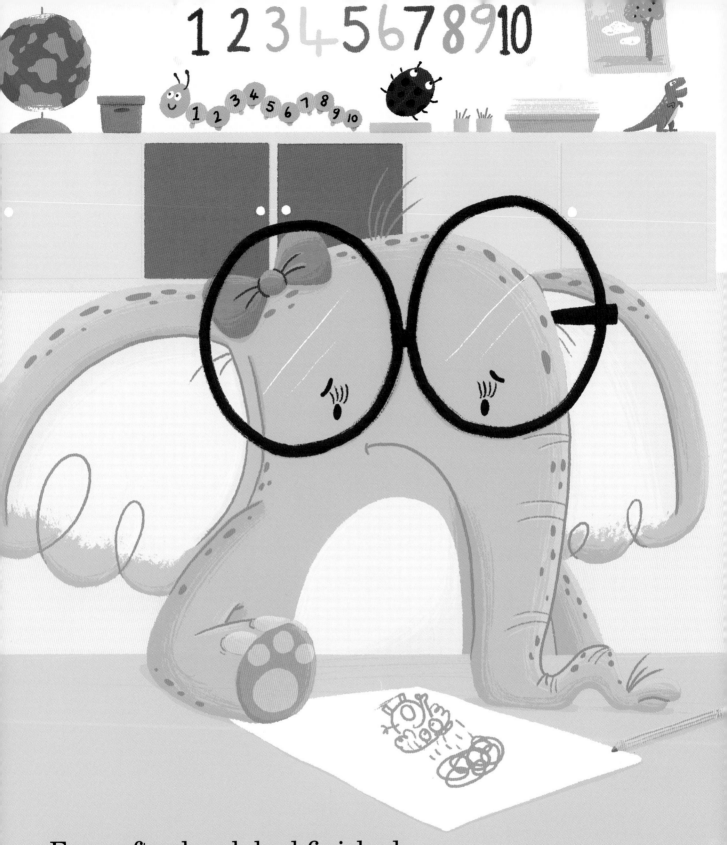

Even after lunch had finished
Things weren't quite the same.
Eppie felt all on her own—
Her allergy to blame.

She couldn't face her playmates.
She could barely even speak.
The fact that they knew her secret
left her feeling small and weak.

When school was finally over,
she didn't say goodbye.
She sidled home—bereft, alone,
and tried hard not to cry.

All throughout that evening,
her thoughts were filled with dread.
They followed her through dinner
and her bath time, straight to bed.

She started the next school day
still feeling lost and all alone.
How would she make it through the day,
with no friends to call her own?

So Eppie didn't look for Allie
when she arrived in class.
She deftly dodged both him and Pearl
and wished the day would pass.

She hid from them at recess,
but peeked as they played ball,
and wondered if her former friends
missed her much at all.

As the time for lunch grew nearer,
she began to fear the worst.
Alone again at lunchtime.
Eppie thought her heart would burst!

She imagined Pearl and Allie
sharing loads of lunchtime fun,
while she sat in the "Nut-Free" zone,
alone and having none.

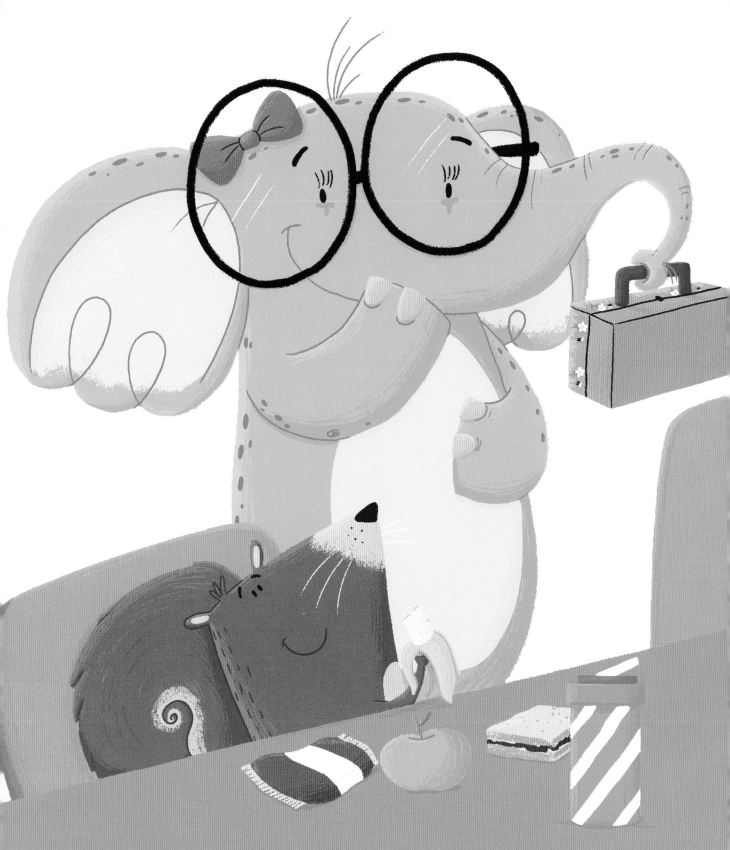

But when she reached her table
the sight that met her eye
made tears of happiness well up.
Yes, big girls sometimes cry.

Because there, side by side,
their smiles of joy full-blown,
sat Eppie's two best buddies
in the distant "Nut-Free" zone.

"Our parents made us tuna,"
said Pearl, with a grin.
"And sorry for laughing," added Allie,
"It won't happen again."

As Eppie stood between them,
they explained how she'd been missed.
They swore they'd make it up to her,
and why she shouldn't resist.

"And we can eat our lunch, each day,
beside this 'Nut-Free' sign!"
Allie and Pearl looked so hopeful,
that Eppie could not decline.

From then on, they were inseparable—
Just Eppie, Allie, and Pearl.
Not a peanut to come between them
and not one care in the world.